WHAT ABOUT THE TOOTH FAIRY?

Elys Dolan

Hodder
Children's
Books

TOOTH
CHUTE

COMING,
TOOTHY!

This is the
TOOTH FAIRY.

And this is her
assistant, Pérez the
TOOTH MOUSE.

The Tooth Fairy and Pérez have a **VERY** important job.

Every night, they pack
up lots of coins and set
off in search of teeth.

They check under
pillows, collecting each
tooth they find . . .

. . . and leaving a
coin in return.

And at the
end of the night,
they take all the
teeth home . . .

...to add to their

MASSIVE CASTLE!

(Yes, it is all made of teeth, but they don't mind that.)

Tooth tree

Tooth Fairy's toothbrush collection

Cheese Plant

Library Tower

World's largest toothbrush

Time for a good clean!

Teeth roof

Teeth walls

Tooth Fairy's room

Pérez's room with cheese and hat collection

Shower Tower

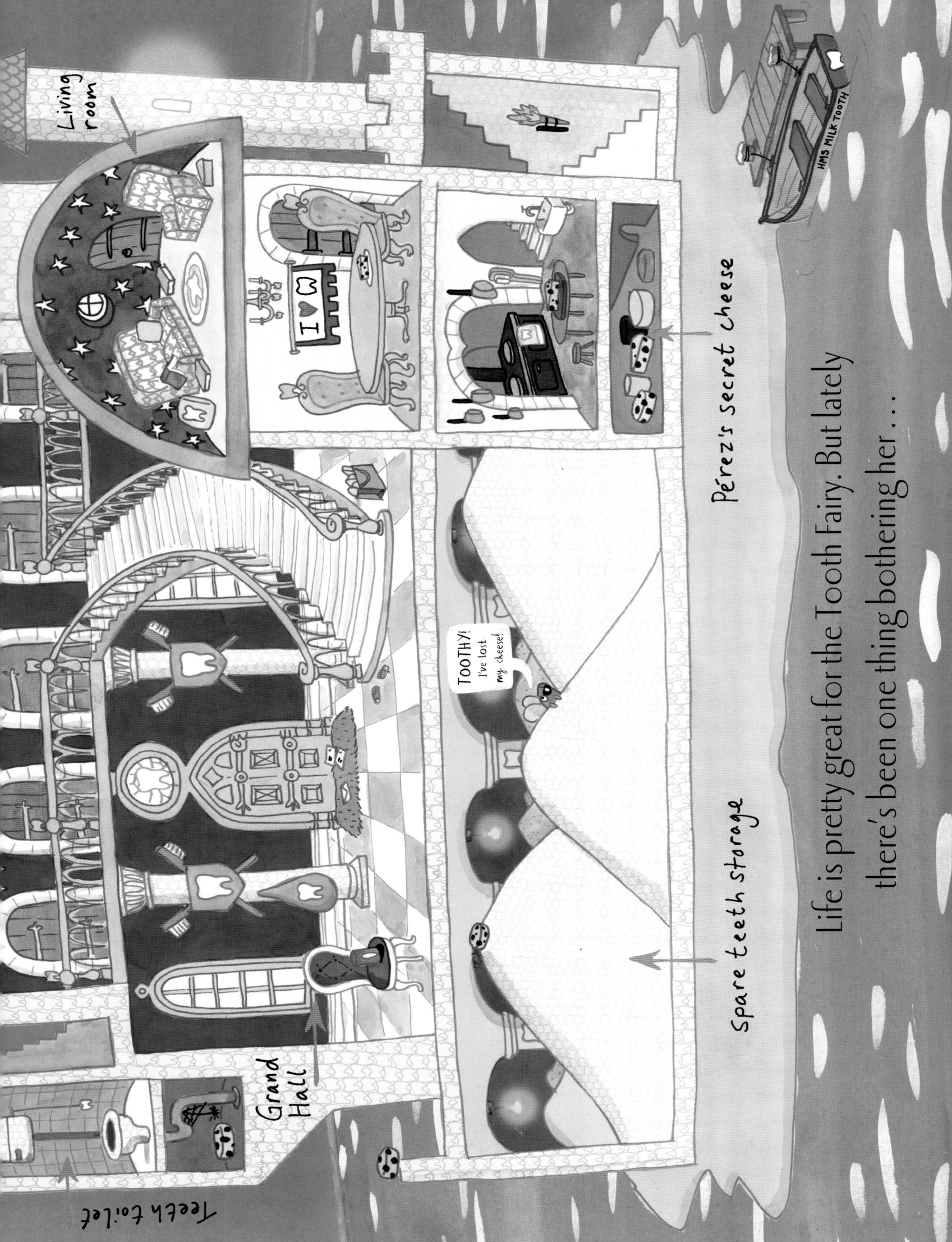

Life is pretty great for the Tooth Fairy. But lately there's been one thing bothering her . . .

Everyone knows **FATHER CHRISTMAS** gets Christmas Day.

The **EASTER BUNNY** has Easter, of course.

Valentine's Day belongs to **CUPID** (who likes people to call him Chad).

Looking good, Chad!

And then there's Halloween, which is run by **JACK O'LANTERN** and his cronies.

"I think you should ask for your **OWN SPECIAL DAY!**" Pérez told the Tooth Fairy.

And that's exactly what she did. The next day, the Tooth Fairy signed up to compete in the

CELEBRATION CHALLENGE.

Children really like what I do, so I think I should have a day too. We can call it TOOTH DAY!

TOOTH DAY EXPLAINED

E. BUNNY

F. CHRISTMAS

Tooth Day? What a ridiculous idea!

SAMPLE

The Celebration Committee were sceptical, but Tooth Fairy was determined. "JUST GIVE ME A CHANCE!"

So they set off to Christmas Town for
the Tooth Fairy's **FIRST** challenge.

CHRISTMAS TOWN

THE
EASTER
PLAINS

VALENTINE'S
BAY

THE
TOOTH
CASTLE

The North Pole

Father Christmas set the **FIRST TASK**.

For a day to be jolly, there must be BEAUTIFUL DECORATIONS of things we all love. Can you decorate a fabulous Christmas tree, Tooth Fairy?

"That's **NOT** jolly, or festive, or even vaguely merry," said Father Christmas. "It's just . . . **WEIRD!** I'm afraid it's a **NO** from me."

But however the Easter Bunny managed to make those eggs,
the Tooth Fairy could not do the same.

"Well that is **NOT** very Easter!" said the Easter Bunny. "It's a **NO**
from me. We'd better move on to the **VALENTINE'S TEST**."

OW!

"Nobody is feeling the love now!" said Chad. "It's a **BIG NO** from me. Get me some hair gel and let's go to the People's Republic of Halloween."

So she left.

Back at the Tooth Castle, the Tooth Fairy went to her bedroom and refused to come out. Pérez missed her a lot.

Pérez knew he wasn't the only one who would miss the Tooth Fairy. The children would still expect their teeth to be collected! So, he put on his angry hat and went to speak to the Celebration Committee.

That night, the Celebration Committee set out to collect the teeth.
But it wasn't the easy job they were expecting . . .

They realised they needed the Tooth Fairy back.

Back in her room, the Tooth Fairy
heard a knock at the door.

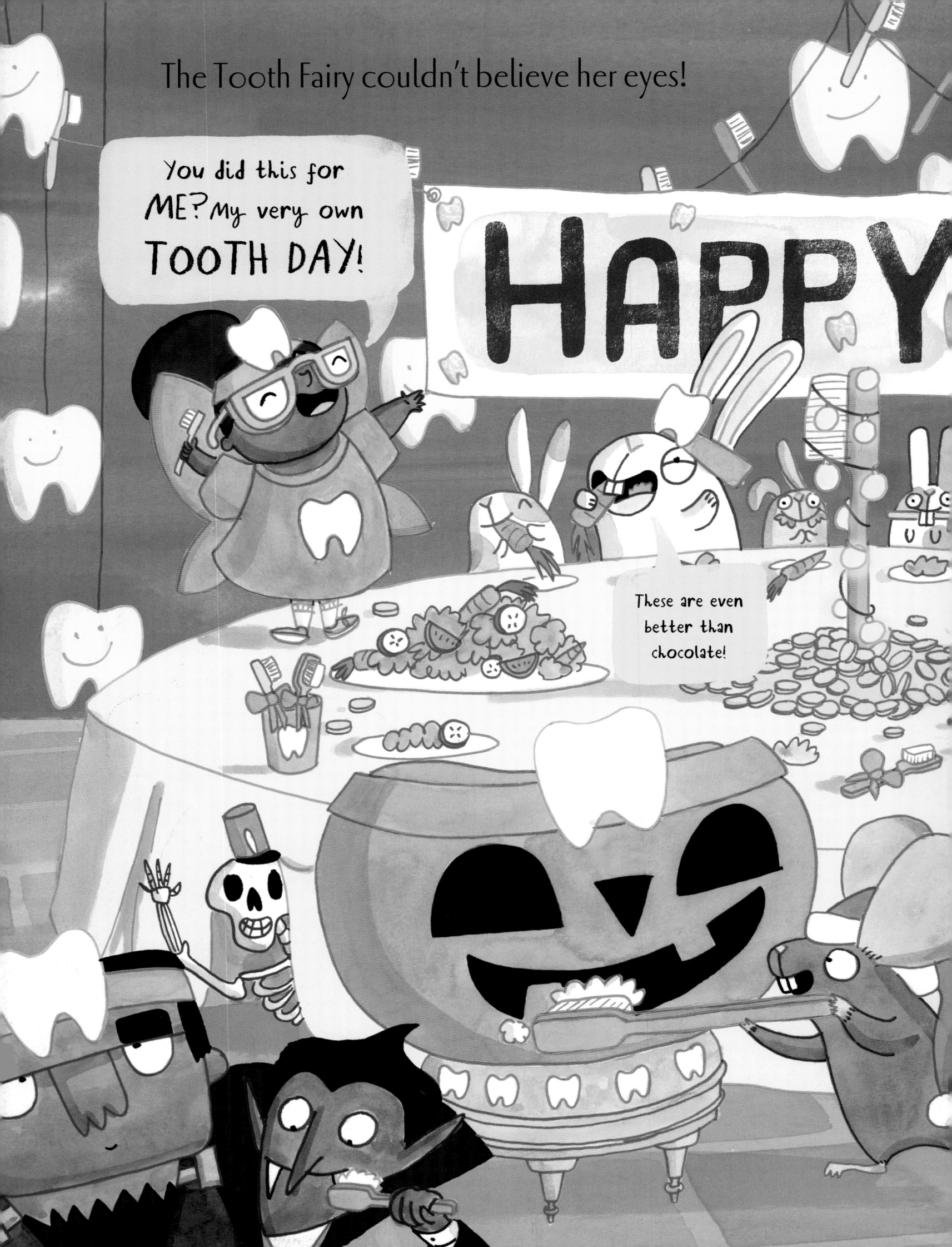

And so, Tooth Day was officially added to the calendar. There was
ONE LAST THING the committee wanted the Tooth Fairy to do . . .